Conversations

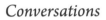

W9-BWJ-125

ALSO BY CÉSAR AIRA FROM NEW DIRECTIONS

Conversations

•

CÉSAR AIRA

Translated by Katherine Silver

A NEW DIRECTIONS PAPERBOOK ORIGINAL

Manufactured in the United States of America
New Directions Books are printed on acid-free paper.
First published as a New Directions Paperbook Original (NDP1294) in 2014
Design by Erik Rieselbach

Library of Congress Cataloging-in-Publication Data
Aira, César, 1949-
[Conversaciones. English]
Conversations / by Cesar Aira ; translated by Katherine Silver.
pages cm
"First published in Spanish as Las conversaciones."
ISBN 978-0-8112-2110-8 (alk. paper)
I. Silver, Katherine, translator. II. Title.
PQ7798.1.I7C6613 2014
863'.64—dc23   2014003892

10 9 8 7 6 5 4 3 2 1

New Directions Books are published for James Laughlin
by New Directions Publishing Corporation
80 Eighth Avenue, New York 10011

CONVERSATIONS

I NO LONGER KNOW IF I EVER FALL ASLEEP. IF I DO, I remain outside of sleep itself, in that constantly moving ring of icy asteroids that circles the dark and immobile hollow of oblivion. It is as if I never enter that shadowy vacuum. I toss and turn, literally, in the zone around it, which is as vast as a world, and actually is the world. I do not lose consciousness. I remain with myself. Thought accompanies me. I don't know if this thought is different from that of full wakefulness; it is, at any rate, very similar.

This is how I spend my nights. To entertain myself, I remember conversations I've had with friends during the day: each night, those of the same day. Every day these conversations give me material for memory. Since I stopped working, I've had nothing better to do than get together with my friends and converse for entire afternoons. I've often wondered if my lack of employment is the reason for my sleep disturbance, because before, when I used to work, I slept normally, like everybody else.

It's quite possible. Deep, restful sleep has always been considered the reward for a productive day. But what choice do I have? I stopped working when my earnings could guarantee me a decent livelihood. Now I have more than enough money to cover my modest necessities, and I have no desire to invent work for myself only to keep busy, as others do. That recourse carries life into the terrain of the unreal, and I am a man of realities. Moreover, work accomplished without any genuine need would fail to fulfill the requirement of tiring me out and allowing me to sleep. The situation would be more readily comprehensible if I were an old man who had given up all activities because of the natural burden of old age, with its ailments and frailties. When I retired early, I found myself at a halfway point; just like with sleep, I cannot ultimately decide whether I am inside or out.

In any case, I am not complaining. Perhaps I really do sleep. The following morning, it is difficult to make that determination. In any case, through the reconstruction of my daily conversations, I have discovered a nocturnal vein of mental activity that is intensely gratifying. At my age, fears of mental decline set in, so it helps to put oneself to the test, to exercise. And this exercise has reassured me that my memory and my ability to focus are still intact, as is my reason.

I am fortunate: throughout my life, I've formed a first-rate circle of friends. Though I myself am not, properly speaking, an intellectual, I've always been interested in and felt affinities for all things cultural; these affinities have translated themselves into close relationships with distinguished personages in the arts, the humanities, and the sciences. They, in turn, have apparently found my company not disagreeable, for the friendships that we've built over time remain strong, and we meet frequently—especially now that I am always available.

The level of our conversations is consistently high. There is no place for gossip, soccer, health issues, or food; our exchanges glide along the lines of history and philosophy. Hence, my nocturnal recollections are rich in sustenance that I can sink my teeth into. The topics we discuss lift them above mere mechanical memory and onto the level of reflection and learning.

In bed, I always focus on the conversations of that same day, though I could also turn my attention to those from years or even decades before. It might sound presumptuous to use the grandiloquent word "memory" for something that occurred no more than a few hours before. But that's fine by me. It is often said that with age, our memory moves further away from the present and that old people are better able to remember what happened in childhood than the day before. I prefer to exercise my memory on what is immediate, closest at hand.

And, truly, my memory is a prodigious apparatus, one that amazes me night after night with its precision and reach. Not only do the topics—and the succession of topics—return, but so do the responses, one by one, and even the uncertainties, our mutterings when we are not able to find the right word, the digressions we allow ourselves. I would like to make clear that our conversations are neither academic nor planned; they are, rather, exchanges among friends (all highly cultured, for sure) with the endless shifts of direction typical of any conversation. Without much effort, I achieve an exact duplicate, though one that is even richer precisely because it is a duplicate. Memory allows me to go more deeply into ideas that pass by too quickly in the course of reality. I can stop wherever I want and contemplate a thought or its expression, analyze the mechanisms that articulate it, discover a defect in an argument, make a correction, retrace certain steps. I look at these conversations, which have become miniaturizations, through a magnifying glass, and my sleepless contemplations render them as beautiful and flawless as jewels. Their very disorder, redundancies, and lack of purpose are swathed in an artistic iridescent sheen because of and thanks to repetition.

Take, for example, my reconstruction last night of the conversation I had yesterday afternoon with one of my friends. We met, as he and I always do, in a café downtown, and while drinking our coffee, we began our dialogue by casually exchanging comments about a movie that had been shown on television the evening before and that we both had happened to see. It was a conventional movie, mere entertainment laced with a few pretensions that did not fool us in the least. My friend and I share the unobjectionable habit of watching banal shows on television at night in order to relax. We also share a distaste for those so-called "cultural" programs that are shown so widely on cable channels. The fact is, the situation of a man of culture is symmetrically inverse to that of the common citizen, who—after a day of prosaic and practical activities—turns on the television set in search of some spiritual elevation. On the contrary, for those of us who have spent our day in the company of Hegel or Dostoyevsky, such "cultural" programs are a waste of time, and for this same reason, as well as their intrinsic worthlessness, we find them paltry and narrow-minded, if not downright ridiculous.

We'd both seen only fragments of this movie; due to tedium and channel surfing as well as domestic distractions, we'd seen different parts, one of us more at the beginning and the other more at the end. But that was enough; stereotypical Hollywood productions of this kind can be fully deduced from one or two scenes, the same way paleontologists can reconstruct an entire dinosaur out of a single vertebra. If one keeps watching, it is only to confirm what one already knows, a confirmation that, difficult as this may be to admit, brings its own satisfaction.

So, we understood each other's comments. Something so trivial, of course, did not call for much commentary on our part, and none would have been made had I not mentioned, with a smile, a fairly gross error that the producers had made. It was as follows: the protagonist, a humble goatherd in the Ukraine ... was wearing a Rolex watch! I burst out laughing when I said it, and when remembering it in bed, a smile surely spread across my face. In the act of doing both things—laughing in reality and smiling upon remembering it—I realized that the blank expression on my friend's face was of someone who doesn't understand what he is hearing. Here it is appropriate to add an aside: a memory can be identical to what is being remembered; at the same time, it is different, without ceasing to be the same. My friend's look of incomprehension, which I saw while sitting across from him at the small table in the café, was precisely that: a request for an explanation that was still unaware that it was requesting one. In my memory, on the other hand, his look was laden with everything that happened subsequently. By virtue of remembering, everything took place at the same time, even though the temporal sequence had been maintained.

I proceeded to explain: the protagonist, at the very moment when he finds one of his goats dead, and bends down to pick it up, precisely at that moment, as he places his hands under the animal's dead body, the sleeve of his coarse, rawhide jacket gets pushed up, exposing his wrist, part of his forearm, and a large gold Rolex watch—clearly recognizable as such with its design and the company's logo: the little crown.

My friend shook himself out of his stupor and asked me: What goat? What dead goat? He had seen no dead goat.

While remembering this, I knew that shortly thereafter we would realize that he had missed that scene. During the conversation itself, that possibility still had not occurred to me, so I tried to help him remember: it was the goat he finds dead when he descends from the mountaintop in the evening, and he carries it to his cabin ... It was impossible that my friend hadn't noticed this episode, because it was important to the storyline, for that night, as he was getting ready to roast the goat for dinner—

That's when he interrupted me: Yes, he'd seen the scene in which he guts the goat, but not the one before that, when he finds it. At that moment, he'd probably gone to the kitchen to get himself something to drink and had missed it. With movies they show on cable channels without commercial interruptions, such gaps were the lesser of two evils and quite common. I surely had similar ones. Everyone does when they watch movies on television. Then the missing scenes return like ghosts: one has to supply them in the imagination in order to complete the story, and then reconstruction and reality— whatever minimal reality those scenes have—get all mixed up.

Once this point had been cleared up, my friend still did not understand what I meant by my observation. What was so weird about the movie's protagonist wearing that watch or any other watch? Don't we ourselves wear watches? he asked, pointing with his chin at the ones we, he and I, had on our left wrists. And we don't wear them for decoration, he added with that smile of his I know so well. We need them so we could meet at the café on time, don't we? This was a self-referentially ironic allusion to his inveterate habit of always arriving late for our dates. I never reproached him. I was so used to it that when we planned to meet I simply added fifteen or twenty minutes to the appointed time; so, one could say that he is very punctual, in a certain sense.

I was obliged to tell him that I was not talking about the watch itself but rather the fact that it was such an elegant one and in possession of an illiterate goatherd, isolated in the mountains. I was also, though, talking about the watch itself. The fact that he had a wristwatch at all was anomalous. That community of goatherds lived in a subsistence economy, completely removed from consumer society. Even assuming that the goatherd would go down to a nearby town for a fair or a market and want to buy himself some object, he would not have chosen a watch, which would have been utterly useless to him. In the ancestral traditions of herdsmen, the only watch that mattered was the Sun. In their world, there were no dates to meet in cafés, no television sets, no trains or airplanes to catch, only the passing of the days and the nights and the seasons. And even in the case that a clever merchant had managed to squeeze a few coins out of this ignorant and innocent mountain dweller, it would have been in exchange for a cheap one, not a Rolex—not even a fake!

The subject had almost run out of steam, as far as I could tell at that moment, and my mind was already groping in other directions, toward the more habitual and usual subjects we discuss, reflections, which we like to delve into, on what we are reading or our thoughts about the world around us. At night, while remembering that point, the subjects that had presented themselves to me as possible, presented themselves again, in their same prenatal condition, without any defined form or content but with the same flavor which had trembled in their imminence—the flavor of philosophy, the intellectual delight of the elite. Perhaps memory enhanced this flavor because in the end these subjects never saw the light of day. What had seemed about to come to an end had, in fact, just barely begun. For a reason I was unable to comprehend, my explanation had not been sufficient; my friend remained perplexed.

Was he distracted, thinking about something else? Or, was it my fault? Had I rushed to my conclusion without allowing enough time for the premises? Had I considered something said that hadn't been? I tried to take stock of the situation as quickly as possible because I felt that the insignificance of the issue called for only a few notes to be touched lightly, without leaning on them, like Arrau playing Schumann. By the same token, if they were too light, things might continue without clarification, and that would be worse. I decided to take one step back and approach the issue from a wider angle—almost as if I were thinking out loud, reviewing it for my own benefit—wanting to avoid that didactic tone that can sound offensive when used to discuss such a trifle.

In the same vein, I spoke about the mistakes that are often made during the making of a movie. They were difficult to avoid, I said, when reconstructing a specific era or environment. One famous example was in *Cleopatra*, in a scene where Elizabeth Taylor, playing the Egyptian queen, wore a dress with a zipper. That was a simple anachronism, not all that different from the aforementioned watch, though in "our" movie, set in the present day, it was a social or socio-cultural discrepancy rather than a temporal one.

With that, I assumed that our little quid pro quo had been resolved, but in order to eliminate any trace of a suspicion that I might have been giving him a lesson or trying to get in the last word, I continued to elaborate, by now in full-blown gratuitous thematic dissipation:

Because of how complicated it is to shoot a movie, the number of people who work on a set and the instructions that have to be given to the technicians and the actors, the director cannot possibly oversee every detail. This is well known and has been for some time, which is why in commercial productions of a certain importance, there are people who specialize in this kind of problem, "continuity people," whose role it is to make sure that the actors wear the same clothes and have the same hairstyle and the same amount of stubble from one day to the next of filming—that everything matches. Because scenes aren't shot in sequence. If a character leaves his house after eating breakfast and saying goodbye to his wife (scene 1), and runs into a neighbor in the street and stops to chat with him (scene 2), those two scenes require different sets, different lighting, and might be filmed weeks apart. But for the character, for the action, only a few seconds have passed, and the clothes and make-up have to be identical ...

With a gesture of impatience, my friend indicated that he already knew all that and suggested I not try to change the subject. That last suggestion came bundled with the previous indication, thanks to the polysemy of gestures, which continued to amaze me while I was remembering them in bed. Because my memories, as I think I have said, are visual as well as auditory. Small appended meanings flourish in the unruffled time of my mind, enriching even further what was already quite rich. As for his impatience, I wasn't worried about that, not in either time frame, for it was not a feeling of being "against" but rather "in favor" of something: I was also constantly expressing the same thing—the eagerness to rid ourselves, as soon as possible, of the static in our communication in order to be able to communicate more fully and take fuller advantage of each other's company. It was more a recognition of the value of one's interlocutor than irritation.

In my memory, that moment was marked by a triumphal blast of imaginary trumpets that announced my friend's entrance into the conversation, for a quick review revealed that until then he had participated with nothing more than a few murmurs, raisings of eyebrows, *whats*, *hows*, *whiches*, and not much more. Now he was ready to talk, and the conversation was set in motion along with the engine of memory.

What he said sounded strange to me. At first, it even greatly perturbed me. During my nocturnal reconstruction, when the weight of that perturbation had lifted, his words were both light and dark. At this third instance, of writing it down, I will try to maintain a balance between the light and the darkness, and my surest guide will be the exact sequence of our exchanges.

All fine and good: he told me that he still did not see the reason for my original remark. He found nothing erroneous about the presence of my famous Rolex on the wrist of the protagonist. As to its price and its condition as a status symbol, he was perfectly aware. Perhaps I didn't know who the actor was. He didn't give me a chance to say that I did know who he was: nothing human is alien to me. Leaning slightly over the table and lowering his voice theatrically, he assured me that this actor had more than enough money to buy himself a Rolex, as well as six more, one for each day of the week, and, if push came to shove, the entire Swiss company that produced them.

And he wasn't exaggerating, he added. I myself had made reference to the complexity of making a movie, a complexity that indicates the magnitude of the enterprise, on which millions, even hundreds of millions of dollars were commonly spent. Now, given the system on which Hollywood bases its audience appeal—the so-called star system—the actors occupy a place of central importance. Movies are marketed using the names of these shining figures that perform in them, and the audience pays its entrance fee to see their extremely well-known faces. That's why they are paid so highly, for their names rather than for the actual work they do—which in the end isn't any different than that of the lowliest electrician, who earns a pittance. This actor in particular was one of those privileged few. He had so much money that he could not possibly live long enough to count it all. True, he acknowledged, taxes take the lion's share, but if one pays them on time, they are never more than a percentage of one's earnings, and no wealthy person has ever become poor from paying them.

Anyway: the several-thousand-dollar watch meant nothing more to him than a cup of coffee meant to us. With this, verisimilitude had been rescued.

Even before I began to think of a reply, and while I was listening to him speak, a vague sensation came over me, the precursor to a much more vigorous one soon to come ... a sensation of strangeness—tinged with a certain amount of disappointment and a remote bit of despair—upon hearing my friend speak so knowledgeably about the world of show business, the money movie stars make, such frivolous nonsense so far beneath the sphere of our interests. It was a nuanced sensation, or one with echoes, because it revealed that I possess that same knowledge. But maybe the modern world is so infused with this information, which is so much a part of even the air we breathe, that it is impossible not to know it.

But when the time came for me to respond, I had to pause. Without realizing it, we had started down a road so subtle that it would carry us from the lowest lows to the highest highs, without many stopovers. The only thing that was obvious, clear as a bell, fit into one very short and very simple sentence: "The actor is not the character." But my intuition clamorously informed me that this generalization was not enough. We were talking about a specific, concrete case, and generalizing would only create a short circuit. I knew I should go back to the beginning, to the Rolex, the goatherd, the mountains, lest I risk tracing a vicious circle of reasoning that would generate still other circles and provide no way out that would allow our conversation to move forward.

Even with these precautions in mind, I had no choice but to begin with a generalization, for otherwise not even I would have understood myself; but I took care to say it in a tone of voice that made clear that I was using it only as a point of departure. The actor, I said, was not the character.

What are you talking about?!

Well, yes ... In a way, he was. The actor continued being the actor while he was playing the character; one could even say that he was more himself than ever, for he was practicing his profession and justifying his existence beyond the good life he led in Beverly Hills, with his divorces and adulteries and consumption of drugs. But a fundamental difference persisted, or better said, emerged. Though fundamental, it was impalpable, perhaps taken for granted with excessive levity. It was "impalpable" (a metaphor I apologized for using and that

I would try to improve upon) because it could be perceived only in the stories and not in the beings that enact them—in the movement of the story itself, not in any one of its moments. Perhaps it should be understood in the same way as the Uncertainty Principle, even if on a different level than that of subatomic particles.

An approving nod from my friend greeted my utterance of the words "different level," which he would repeat shortly. I continued:

A successful Hollywood heartthrob, I said, had enough money to buy himself an expensive Swiss watch, just as a woman in the second half of the twentieth century wore dresses with zippers. Those were their stories, or lack of stories. The imperative that prevented a primitive goatherd in the remote mountains of Ukraine from wearing a Rolex was almost as powerful as that which prevented an Egyptian queen of the first century from wearing a dress with a zipper. So, a Hollywood heartthrob and a Ukrainian goatherd on the one hand, and a modern woman and the Queen of the Nile on the other: were they the same person? Apparently, they could not be, at least not on the same level. "Level" of course is also a metaphor, and also in this instance I intended to distance myself from it, and to do so right away, because the other level was that of fiction, which was not a metaphor but rather, in a way, the real—perfectly real—lifeblood of all metaphors. Fiction created a second and simultaneous world . . .

Here I interrupted myself twice over. I did so in the conversation, because I could see that I was getting nowhere, and I did so when I was remembering the scene of the conversation, because I saw that I was reaching my goal too quickly. The impetus to speak and to remember what was spoken, though the same, were charged with distinct and incompatible energies.

We had the actor, the beautiful and famous blond in his mansion in Southern California, with his numerous bank accounts, his expensive watches, his swimming pool, his Ferrari, his top-model girlfriends. His agent called him and told him that a big studio was offering him the starring role in a new movie by a prestigious director, and that they had agreed without a murmur to his multi-million dollar fee. There was no reason to say no a priori. What was it about? What would be his role? It was an adventure movie that took place in the mountainous desert region of Ukraine, and its plot dealt with aspects of the sudden advent of capitalism in the republics of the former Soviet Union. He would play the role of a primitive goatherd, far removed from modern civilization, a kind of noble savage, who suddenly sees himself involved in a sinister plot . . . Anyway, something more or less predictable, with just enough originality to justify making the movie, but not too much to scare off the audience. And it behooved him to take the role because it would give him opportunities to shine, as well as a temporary reprieve from the string of urban, yuppie, fashion-police roles that he'd been playing for the last few years. In short: a renewal of his image, replete with the shaggy beard he would let grow, long hair, troglodyte garb; and his agent didn't need to tell him, because he knew it all too well, that he would look fabulous in all of it, that his shaggy beard would be groomed by a hairdresser to the stars, and his rawhide garments would be fashioned by the best designer available.

The actor was able to ascertain the potential for all these benefits a few days later when he read the screenplay they sent him. He read it in the enormous living room of his house, reclining in an armchair, with a large Portuguese water dog sleeping on the rug at his feet, in that light sleep animals enjoy: each time a page turned, there was just enough noise to make the ears of his loyal Bob twitch. I could picture the scene perfectly when I was describing it to my friend, and much better when I relived the conversation at night — so much better, that I no longer heard the words: I just saw what they evoked.

That screenplay, I continued, was "fictional," which meant that it told a story that had never taken place. It hadn't taken place in reality, the proof of which was that at the moment it was being written, it could still have turned out to be something else: the story of a failed marriage, a robbery, an invasion of extraterrestrials, the life of the pope, or the inventor of the microwave oven. But, no: out of the almost infinite combinations of possible situations, the one that had come into being was that of a goatherd ... And we already knew the rest.

This was the plot of the movie that was made. The production team traveled to Ukraine to find the right locations, and when everything was just about ready to be filmed, there went our heartthrob—in the meantime he had had time to let his hair and beard grow and to conscientiously study his role.

It's not that they couldn't have filmed it in a studio in Los Angeles. Everything can be reproduced on a set with the right staging and a few editing tricks. If they wanted the real mountains, all they had to do was send a cameraman there and then insert those takes where they belonged. But the decision to film on location was the result of the producers' well-reasoned policy, which took into account several concurrent factors, the first being financial, for the cost of living in Ukraine was exponentially less than in the United States, and the salaries of the people they'd hire in situ would allow them to significantly reduce their budget; moreover, the Ukrainian authorities showed interest in the project, which fit in with their own policy of attracting strategic investments; with the Ministry of Culture's cooperation, they would be allowed to shoot interior spaces normally off limits to the public, thereby exhibiting to the world the country's unknown artistic and architectural riches; finally, there was the famous quality of light in the mountains, which would give the film its own, unique atmosphere, which could not be reproduced by artificial means.

In any case, there went the actor. Needless to say, he did not go alone; he took his secretary, bodyguards, assistants, a coach, and a personal trainer. Nor did he pack his own bags, also needless to say, for that's what he paid his servants to do, but he did choose certain objects or items of clothing that he wanted to take with him. One of those objects was the watch. He opened his dresser drawer where he kept watches and jewelry, quickly thought out what he would need and what would be convenient to have (this was not the first time he had traveled to film in exotic locations), and he chose his solid and reliable gold Rolex Daytona. This reliable timepiece served various purposes. In the first place, a watch — which he had little use for in the course of his pampered life — was indispensable during those frenetic days of shooting out in nature, as he well knew from experience: risings at dawn, constant moves from place to place, last-minute changes of plans, urgent meetings. Moreover and by the same token, the watch for such circumstances should be water and shock resistant, for he didn't know what ordeals it would have to endure. At the same time, he wanted it to be elegant, an expression of his stature as a sex symbol and a man of success, for the shooting of the film would entail more than just acting: there would be parties, outings, and they had even planned ahead for public relations events with the Ukrainian authorities, who — he could bet on it — would want to have their pictures taken with him.

I was putting a lot of my own into all this, but it is natural to put into any story, along with a lot of what one has seen and heard, assumptions of cause and effect, without which there are too many loose ends. I was a little ashamed to expose how much I knew about the life and work of movie stars, for it might lead one to think that I was especially interested in the subject or that I wasted my time reading "special interest" magazines. But, as I already said, knowledge of these popular subjects is in the air, and an effort must be made to not acquire it rather than to acquire it. And, as I also already said, nothing human is alien to me. Knowing does not occupy much room: information about actors or singers does not take space away from Plato or Nietzsche. I've always distrusted those intellectuals who have never heard of the Rolling Stones. My friend and I saw eye to eye on this; just a few minutes earlier, he had talked knowledgeably about the "star system," by way of example.

Our actor did not travel directly there. He stopped off in Paris, where he met with his co-star and the producers, and together they gave a press conference to announce the project. This event took place in the ballroom of a large hotel in the French capital; he was besieged by flashes from photographers, eager to publicize his change of "look" (hair and beard): he was beginning to turn into the primitive herdsman of the movie, even though he was still himself. And he was so much himself that he wound up getting annoyed at the journalists' insistence on asking about his recent divorce and the beautiful actress who had precipitated it. Nor was he pleased with their political questions about the collaboration implied by his participation in this movie with the governments of the countries in the ex-Soviet Bloc, governments he had criticized during his period of environmental activism.

The order of my reasoning was implacable. One by one I was introducing all the elements for a proof of reality, which I could then use when I contrasted it with fiction. While I was reconstructing the conversation (and there, also, I was implacable in not skipping a single word, and I might have even added a few), I realized that the "actor" was already the "character" in a certain sense: not the character that he would soon embody during the shooting of the movie, but the character of the story that I, marginally and for the rhetorical imperatives of the demonstration, was recounting. And the more details I added in order to round out the figure of the "actor," the more of a "character" he became. This was inevitable, for fiction, in order to express itself, adopts a narrative structure that is the same as the one used by reality to make itself intelligible. Inevitable or not, however, I had to admit that it weakened my argument. It would have benefited, for instance, from a stronger contrast, from the positing of a reality that my friend and I would recognize as more real—for example, our own reality or something equivalent. The reality of a Hollywood star was colored by unreality and not easy to take seriously.

Even so, I believed I was on the right track, and I continued: we were already in the Desert Mountains, and here all we needed to do was take a quick look at the process of making the movie: the long days of filming when the lighting was good, the changes of location for scenes that took place in villages or the city, the endless repetitions demanded by the director who was a perfectionist, the inevitable interruptions due to rain or problems with the team or the local extras not keeping to the schedule. We might also pass over the no less important editing process carried out in studios back in Los Angeles. We then came to what we had watched the night before on our television sets: the story of a goatherd who was a victim of circumstance. That character didn't exist and never had. The identification between him and the actor who had given him body and voice was momentary and functional. Once the movie was made, the actor could forget about him forever. The goatherd (the "character") was a fantasy created for artistic and commercial purposes—much more the second than the first in this case—a fantasy made of images and words, whose precarious reality was at the mercy of the movie lovers' voluntary suspension of disbelief. A fundamental difference resided in the fact that the life of the actor was biological, it had a long "before"—as seen from his screen career, his divorce, his dog Bob—and would have an "after" that would last as long as Destiny provided; whereas the goatherd would continue to repeat that illusory fragment of nonbiological life, made of light and electronic impulses. They had coincided only in representation.

But, with all the precariousness of his illusory existence, the goatherd also had to have a backstory, and though fictitious, that story had to be somehow "more," that is, it had to be more intelligible than real stories, which unfold in a chaos of happenstance and twists and turns. To do this, it had to emphasize one aspect that real stories also contain: verisimilitude. This is a conventional term that includes everything mankind does in its perennial war against the absurd. In reality, there are things in any given context that cannot happen. I used as an example our "reality witness," the life of the blond movie star: we would never see him standing at the door of a church in Beverly Hills asking for spare change, would we?

My friend raised his eyebrows and looked slightly skeptical, which I had been expecting.

Yes, we might see him there, if it were a joke or because he had lost a bet, or even as the result of a rapid decline due to drug and alcohol abuse. Stranger things have happened. But it was precisely the emphasis on the verisimilar I had mentioned earlier that made it impossible in fiction. A goatherd who had always lived in the mountains, who had never stepped foot in a city, who ate whatever the earth provided, that nonexistent goatherd, created by the imagination, his life circumscribed to an hour and a half of pulses of light and color, had to maintain complete factual coherence in order to remain plausible. Above all, he should not be confounded with the actor who was playing him. For example, as he was gathering his flock before descending the mountain in the evening, he couldn't suddenly burst out with a sentence like: "Come on, hurry up, I'm having dinner with Madonna tonight." Even if it were true that the actor was having dinner with Madonna that night, that sentence would be out of place in the character's mouth. Indeed, out of place in exactly the same way as the presence of a Rolex on his wrist was out of place.

But, if it was impossible, how did it come about? Here, I said, we required the intervention of the imperfection that accompanies every human endeavor. It was a mistake, the result of a momentary distraction, a small error that escaped the vigilance of all involved, who were legion. To a certain extent it was understandable, given the complexity of a movie production of that size. The night scene shot on the mountainside with a dead goat; the crew measuring the light levels, the angles; making sure the cameras were functioning; the various scenes being filmed discontinuously ... The actor, who'd completely forgotten about his watch, was focused on the action, on showing his own best angle ... Anyway, that's what had happened, there was nothing more to say about it.

To my surprise, my friend remained unconvinced. Moreover, he emphatically informed me—with that momentum typical of someone who has been waiting for the other person to finish talking in order to express their own opposing opinion—that my interpretation of the movie was completely wrong.

I answered simply that I had not offered an interpretation of the whole movie, which I had watched in fits and starts and without paying much attention. I was merely pointing out a single error.

He had not watched more of it or with more attention than I had, he said, the proof of which was that he hadn't even seen the famous night scene with the dead goat. Hence, he also would not risk an interpretation, but he did feel he was in a position to refute me.

I had the irrepressible suspicion that he was going to come out with something very off the wall; surprise gave way to deep fear. One's social life is full of such fears, and each person reacts to them according to his character. My character is rather shy, defensive, with an excess of politeness that renders me almost pusillanimous. I am one of those people who places delicacy above all other considerations and who discovers, time and time again, that cut-and-dry cruelty at the right moments can save many other moments of unpleasantness, but I never learn. I am also one of those people who prefers to live an entire life with a lie than live one uncomfortable moment of truth.

What I feared in this case (and by "this case" I meant the occasion in the café as well as its expansion in my memory when I relived the scene in the darkness of my bedroom in the middle of the night) was that my friend would utter a couple of sentences, a couple of words—he didn't need many—that would show me that he was a complete and utterly hopeless idiot. Because the point of our little disagreement was so obvious as to be beyond any discussion. "The actor is not the character." Who could deny that? Only someone with the mental level of a four-year-old child—and even a child that age would not be difficult to convince. In fact, it was not a matter of convincing him but merely giving him time to see it; only a momentary mental lapse, distraction, or partial deafness while listening to the proposition could leave room for doubt.

The fault was mine. I had asked for it by launching into a long harangue full of subtleties and philosophical consider-ations instead of limiting myself to the basics and letting him see it. I had done this out of intellectual vanity—the plea-sure of hearing myself talk; inevitably it ended up complicat-ing what was simple, muddling what was clear. If now it was shown—as seemed imminent—that he had not seen the ob-vious, I would be left dangling over an abyss, weighed down by all my verbiage.

Deep down it didn't much matter if my explanation had been long or short, except that by making it long, I had cre-ated greater expectations and exposed myself to more seri-ous disappointment: if he did not understand the difference between the actor and the character in a movie, he was an imbecile. And if he was an imbecile, I had no choice but to lose all intellectual respect for him and, which was worse, it meant that our conversations were wiped out as far as everything about them that was good and gratifying for me. Not only would I lose them in the future—for I would necessarily lose all desire to bring up interesting subjects or share intelligent reflections with a fool of that caliber—but I would retrospectively lose the conversations that we'd held throughout the years and that constituted such a central part of my life. This revelation detracted from the past—its richness became fictitious—and created a gaping hole that would be difficult to fill. How to fill a hole in the past from the present? My conversations themselves were somewhat retrospective. The nocturnal reconstructions I put them through—no less important a part of the pleasure they gave me—displaced them in time even while they were occurring; the second time contaminated the first and thereby a circle was drawn. I had been living in that magic circle, protected by its circumference, and its dissolution filled me with dread.

In order to appreciate the magnitude of my disappointment, I should explain just how important conversations are for me. At this stage of my life, they have become the single most important thing. I have allowed them to occupy this privileged position, and have cultivated them as a raison d'être, almost like my life work. They constitute my only worthwhile occupation, and I have devoted myself to enhancing their value, treasuring them through their reconstruction and miniaturization on my secret nocturnal altar. Hence, if I lose the day, I also lose the night. In fact, my nights even more than my days would be emptied out, for it is always possible to find other distractions during the day; nights are more demanding; their entire sustenance is intelligence and the complicity of intelligence, which becomes complicity with myself through my system of duplication. To lose that would be to lose myself, to remain alone in my aimless insomnia.

It's true, he was not my only friend nor my only conversational partner. He was one among many—I did not value him above the others. But it would be a loss that would go beyond the unit he represented. In my relationships with my friends, I have noticed—and I think this must be a universal phenomenon—that each one is regulated by a distinct line of interests, a distinct tone of friendship, even a different language. Friends are not interchangeable, even when the degree of friendship is the same and the level of culture and social standing is equivalent. There are unspoken understandings and agreements and codes that are built up over time and that make each one irreplaceable. But the loss, as I said, would go beyond what was unique. The conversations from which I derive so much pleasure form a system, and the disappearance of that "vein" of topics or shared opinions with this friend would create an imbalance, and this in turn would lead to the collapse of the entire network.

Nevertheless, beneath these fears, a doubt remained, the same one that had led to my initial surprise: Was this possible? Wasn't it a bit excessive? The contrast between my educated and civilized friend and the ignorance of a person thus impaired was almost supernatural. Shouldn't he be above such suspicions? Had he not given me sufficient proof, throughout the years, of his intelligence and perceptiveness? I had lost count of the number of times we had discussed, as equals, philosophers and artists and social and historical phenomena. My trust in his responses never flagged. And I was not under some kind of illusion, of this I could be certain, for I had submitted each conversation to the nocturnal test of memory, and I had scrutinized every last crease. During these reconstructions, I even scrutinized what had not been said. This discovery, if that is what it was, would be like suddenly discovering, after years of a relationship, that a friend had only one arm, or not even, because a one-armed man can hide his handicap with a prosthetic arm; to refine the simile, it would be more like a man discovering, while celebrating his silver wedding anniversary, that his wife was Chinese. Was that possible? Unfortunately, I had to respond in the affirmative. It was possible. In this case, evidence didn't help; the strength of the unexpected destroyed it.

Nor did it help me to consider this as one of those blanks we all have in our education and that are sometimes as scandalous and as shocking as the one I was confronting at this moment. It had happened to me before, that I believed I knew something without knowing it because as a child I had adopted an erroneous idea about it, which worked well enough to never have felt the need to revise it or put it to the test. Due to extremely long concatenations of happenstance, one might never come across certain subjects, even when in possession of an alert mind and universal curiosity. This is possible because there are so many. Sometimes it is a question of pure laziness. For example, I know that there is an explanation for the fact that stagecoach wheels in Westerns appear to be turning backwards when the vehicle is moving quickly forward; I have even seen it written up and illustrated with diagrams, but I never bothered finding out about it in more detail. To have one of these gaps of comprehension or information is the most common thing in the world; however, this didn't do me any good here, because the difference between fiction and reality was not an isolated issue that could reside in a blind spot; it was instead an oil spill, which spread over everything, even over what surrounded everything.

Someone less generous or more aggressive might have been pleased to discover that a friend of his was stupid. It would make him feel superior, safe in his narcissistic integrity, more intelligent than he thought: in a word, the winner. This was not the case for me. I felt depressed and distressed, like someone on the verge of losing something of great value. In reality, that feeling lasted a few seconds, the time that elapsed between one remark and another in an animated dialogue. In bed at night, I wondered: can depression last a few seconds? Apparently, this was not a true depression but rather its conceptual nucleus, suitable to expand upon in memory, and I tried, almost as if it were a game, to do so in order to delight in its contemplation. As my memory already knew that there was no reason to be depressed, I did so in "fictional" mode, establishing a bridge between the subject and its development.

As I said, my friend's reply was unexpected; he had been champing at the bit and bringing to bear all his patience so as not to interrupt me. He showed no sign of lack of comprehension or confusion; on the contrary: he was determined to free me from my error.

He started by saying something that I took as a somewhat marginal generalization. According to him, actor and character could coexist, and the movie we had both watched proved this; if I had really watched it, he added with a touch of sarcasm, because the scope of my error made him doubt that I had. In order for them to coexist, neither a suspension of skepticism nor any other psychological or metaphysical operation was necessary, as I had proposed in my ravings, but only a bit of ingenuity. Ingenuity in invention, occupational ingenuity, perhaps not a lot, only the usual for this kind of artistic-commercial production; he was not sufficiently familiar with what was currently going on in Hollywood to evaluate what we had seen: it could be a product off the movie assembly line, no different from the hundred or thousand others churned out each year by the dream factory, or it could be a movie that just happened to turn out really good.

On the same subject, he made a digression in order to explain that he did not feel comfortable in the discussion on which we had embarked. His mind, trained in philosophy, could be applied only with violent effort to a subject as banal as Hollywood fluff. He did not know the codes of what came under the heading "mass entertainment," and he feared he would commit errors of evaluation, not only of the quality, as he had mentioned earlier, but even of the meaning itself. At the same time, he admitted that no object was too small for an inquisitive mind.

I agreed, and when I remembered the words I used to tell him so, I also remembered, in a blinding flash, my years of practice in conversation, which was a grand object, capacious enough to hold cultural profundities, yet also small and minimal in its parts and in the parts of its parts: everything, the small and the large, had been bathed in the same impartial light of repetition.

He warned me that he would have to make certain assumptions, some of them quite risky.

Go ahead, I said.

In order for what we were doing to not seem like a dialogue of the deaf, he began, he would start with my ideas in the hope of getting me to see the flip side.

I had spoken of verisimilitude, right? In fact, I had based my argument on it. That it was not verisimilar for a humble mountain herdsman to be wearing a fancy Rolex. So, if ours had one, this would create a rupture in verisimilitude, and there my syllogism ended.

I thought that it wasn't that simple, or at least I had made it not that simple because I had gone back to the root of the problem, but at that moment I didn't feel like arguing (perhaps due to the residual effect of my super-brief depression), and I wanted to see where he was going, so I merely assented with a quick nod of impatience. Anyway, if we were perfectly frank, it *was* that simple.

Hence, he continued, my error consisted of me having limited myself to a static concept of verisimilitude. He proposed a different, more dynamic one. According to this concept, and seen within the movement of creation, verisimilitude could be, and was, a generator of stories. That attribute was a by-product of its very raison d'être, which was to rectify an error. A real or virtual error, because it didn't matter that one had not been committed or that never in a million years would it have crossed the mind of the author to commit it: the possibility of the error or anachronism or nonsense was enough, and the authors of stories, even if they didn't know it, cultivated this possibility, protected it, and treasured it as their most precious asset.

With one wave of his hand, he silenced my request for an explanation, even if one was not necessarily forthcoming (I didn't even know if it was).

We had to go a little further back, he said, to focus in on the question. Stories that are told or written or filmed, whether they belong to the realm of reality or fiction, have to have qualities that make them worthwhile, because they are neither facts nor natural occurrences. A rock along the side of the road, or a cloud, or a planet does not need to justify itself with its beauty or interest or novelty, but a story does. Because stories are gratuitous and have no specific function, other than whiling away the time, they rely on their quality. Inventiveness has to be maximized in each instance: each time, a new rabbit has to be pulled out of the hat. One recourse they use is verisimilitude. But not a static and narrow verisimilitude, which reality itself provides, but rather "emergency" verisimilitude, the one that arrives at the last minute, like firefighters with their sirens blaring, coming to the rescue in a dangerous situation.

Once he had established that premise, he returned to me. I was wrong to consider the Rolex an error or an anachronism or the result of a momentary oversight during the filming. Completely wrong. But even so, it could be considered a "possible" error, that is, posited as an error in the original generation of the story. This was not difficult to do. I had already thoroughly outlined the conditions for doing so: where was a primitive goatherd in the mountains of Ukraine going to get a Rolex? All fine and good. But if the goatherd in the story had a Rolex, and we had posited that the "error" had been committed, it had to be fixed, that is, made verisimilar. The story's interest and novelty would emerge from such an operation. Only then would the story be rendered worthwhile. Without the "error," things narrowed considerably. Who would be interested in the coherent life of a goatherd? Or of a coherent tycoon with a big gold watch? The interest arose, a priori, from their coexistence.

How could the Rolex on the goatherd's wrist be justified? This was not so difficult. Here the author might regret that the "error" had not been more serious, for example, that the goatherd, who walked through the mountains along rocky paths only passable by goats . . . had a Ferrari! That would have demanded a much broader expansion of verisimilitude and would have resulted in a much more interesting story, right?

He paused after that little rhetorical question, which was not even that but rather a linguistic tic of his with which I was very familiar. So familiar that it didn't even register in the conversation; but it did reappear when I laid it out on the table of my dreams. Which made me think, or rather feel, that there was something in my nocturnal reconstructions that surpassed me.

He gazed off into the distance, though he did not pause for long, for he already knew what he was going to say next. Maybe he paused only for effect.

In the meantime, in bed I used this opportunity to pause, even though I could do so whenever I wanted, between any question and any response, or, if I felt like it, if an idea suddenly struck me, in the middle of a sentence, and even in the middle of a word. During my pause I thought of something I should have thought of during his pause (during mine, it became an anachronism): up to this point his reasoning had been subtle and intelligent, which reassured me as far as my previous fears went: he was not a complete idiot, not at all. He was earning a lot of credit, and he even seemed poised to pay off his debt in full. Although it was also true that not being an idiot didn't prevent him from being something even worse—for example, a madman. But I didn't elaborate on that; I had more realistic things to think about. Anyway, he was already moving on.

How, then, to justify the Rolex on the wrist of the goat-herd? How to justify it, not from the point of view of the spectator (from which, as I had shown, it was unjustifiable), but rather from that of the creator of the story? Very easily. It was clear as a bell. He had to become a fake goatherd. For example, a millionaire who was renouncing his millions because he was sick and tired of civilization and had gone into the mountains to live in communion with nature, or an undercover spy from the CIA trying to find out the secret route of the Baku-Kiev pipeline, or a fugitive from justice, or a scientist studying the behavior of goats ... A full range of possibilities fanned open, though it would quickly start to close under pressure from the inflexible stipulations of realism.

Even when the fan was fully open, he said, certain restrictions appeared and began to leave clues. The distance between the Rolex and the traditional goatherd was one. The distance, more literally, between the centers of civilization, where people might wear Rolex watches, and remote mountaintops was another. Both coincided to indicate that the issue held a certain "importance." Nobody, just for the sake of it, renounced the benefits of creature comforts to suffer the harsh conditions of life in the mountains, especially if they had the means to pay for those comforts, which was the case of anyone who owned a watch for the rich. There had to be a weighty reason. The arc traced by the fan, now narrower, was still extended over a broad area. In order to keep reducing it, one could turn—and this was a prudent step to take—to the genre the story was going to serve. A serious novel was not the same as a comic strip, and a surrealist story was not a ninja movie. Here we were dealing with a movie that belonged to the category "action and adventure thriller," with a political backdrop. Once we had made this determination, we would need to look at the catalog of the more or less recent productions in this genre and try to find something that had not yet been done. Since we were within the rubric of commercial movies for mass consumption, it was better not to be overly original, for this could carry it over to the eccentric and thereby limit the target audience. Originality should not go beyond the conventional, right?

But to get to the subject at hand, he continued, we already had the North American hero on his way to the problematic highlands of Crimea on a secret mission. The choice of location was dictated by several considerations, which in turn dictated others, and with all of them combined, the story was well on its way.

Ever since the collapse of the Soviet Bloc, Ukraine had been showing signs of wanting to distance itself from Russia. The strong lobby of the pig-iron oligarchy was pressing for greater independence from Moscow in their negotiations over the price of their exports. Putin, in turn, was applying pressure by threatening to cut off energy supplies. The internal situation was becoming increasingly complicated due to longstanding ethnic conflicts. The hatred between the Tatars and the Cossacks, kept latent for centuries by the exclusion of the former in 1590, had resurged explosively after the annexation of Crimea in the 1960s. A Tatar population had been preserved intact on the peninsula, which, due to contact with the progressive strands of Yeltsinism via tourism, now called itself neo-Tatar and denounced the past and present discriminatory policies of the influential Moldovan and Lithuanian minorities. The Ukrainian racial cauldron, stirred up by the presumptuousness of the Polish aristocracy and the deviousness of Romanian intellectuals, fugitives from Ceauşescu's dungeons, led to the emergence of a new class of political opportunists. Using modernization as an excuse, a demagogic Legislature approved a request for numerous loans from the IMF and the World Bank. Washington was watching with interest, speculating about the emergence of a strategic ally in the region. Ever since the end of the Cold War, the Empire had been embarked on the somewhat paradoxical mission of increasing the reach of globalization. The opportunity to stake out some territory presented itself to them with the case of the toxic algae and Señorita Wild Savage.

A topographical question that was worth addressing before moving on to "your precious Rolex," he said with a smile, was the following: all of Ukraine was an immense plain of black soil atop the Podolian Uplands, which leaned gently toward the Caspian Sea. All of its two hundred thousand square miles were arable, making the country a grain producer of the first magnitude. Across this gigantic plateau ran the three national rivers—the Dnieper, the Dniester, and the Dnierer. Irrigated by the waters of these rivers, the land flourished with alfalfa, which fed the cattle, another source of the country's wealth.

Anyway, given all this, where were the mountains, those mountains that were from time immemorial the site of Ukrainian legends, the famous mountains of coal inhabited by nocturnal demons and hermits and lost races and eyeless beasts? Where were they?

The case of the toxic algae addressed this question with striking precision. These extremely dangerous mutated marine growths had recently appeared in the depth of the Caspian Sea, so deep in its trenches that nobody could see them. Their existence and characteristics had to be deduced from the mortality of deep-sea fish that appeared, floating belly-up, in the surf—fish that were themselves unknown till then.

The ichthyologists who identified and studied them found in their intestinal tracts microscopic fragments, sometimes only a few loose cells, of the algae that had killed them. From those minimal traces, they could diagram the algae.

Then, by simply applying a well-known fact, algae that made their home in the depths of the sea should also be found on the mountains peaks. With this, their existence was definitively confirmed.

Here my friend quickly shifted gears and launched right into the next subject, eager as he was to arrive at "my Rolex," which he must have by now sighted on the horizon from the crest of the argumentative wave he was riding:

Señorita Wild Savage—

But I cut him off sharply with speech and gestures. I threw myself back in my chair and shot both hands in the air, as if I were climbing a wall.

Just one moment!

I sighed deeply, and upon remembering it in bed, I couldn't resist sighing more weakly, in a kind of mock-up of the one I had released in the café.

How could you keep going, I asked, by using such a crass parody of a syllogism as a bridge? I was sorry to have to disillusion him, but as far as I was concerned the mountains still did not exist.

He retraced his steps without his feathers getting the least bit ruffled: didn't I know that geologists had deduced important information about the planet's past from fossils of marine animals found on high mountain peaks?

Of course I knew that. But that didn't make mountains rise!

I agree, he said, it didn't make them rise ... in reality. But we had already made clear, or better said, I had made clear, abundantly and effectively, if not excessively, that there is a difference between fiction and reality. And we were in the realm of fiction, right? I myself had said as much, he wasn't inventing anything. In any case, he had merely fine-tuned it: the terrain on which we were moving was not that of fiction already made and consumed like a bowl of popcorn, but rather of its generation. And in this terrain, which now was becoming metaphoric, the mountains did actually rise out of what I scornfully called a "parody of a syllogism." Above all, I should kindly remember that the fiction genre we were discussing was that of entertainment for mass consumption. Even children know the fact about marine fossils on mountain peaks. Moreover, it is the kind of information that, outside the restricted world of professional geologists, holds interest *only* for children. But adults were once children, and they remember. The popular culture industry is built on such memories.

I continued to resist. While remembering the conversation, I already knew what came next: Señorita Wild Savage. In the conversation itself I probably also knew, because he had already spoken her name, but in my memory, Señorita Wild Savage rose up in me like a tide of magnetized currents that swept me away into adventure, youth, the world of passions. This is why I paused with particular complacency on the objection I now presented, and on his response:

How is it possible, I asked him, that the inopportune mutation of algae could have been contemporaneous with fossils that must have been millions of years old?

Another "little anachronism," right? he replied with an astute smile that indicated that he had been expecting that objection and was grateful for it. In effect, it was another one of those errors that required the labor of verisimilization. The fact that the algae had recently mutated did not mean that they hadn't existed since ancient times; rather, since then they had contained, latently, the very mechanisms that would make the mutation possible. For an experienced paleobiologist, those mechanisms would be visible in the fossils, and studying them would not only lead to a greater understanding of genetic history but also help deal with the threats posed to life forms in the present day.

But this was a very narrow, very functional verisimilization. There were other, better ones, and if I had the patience to listen, he would elucidate the situation.

Aria was a beautiful young Tatar woman, secretary of the Pig-Iron Foundation, whose president the sinister Forion Larionov had become after the death of the previous president, a kindhearted gentleman and Aria's uncle. She suspected that the accident that had taken her uncle's life had not really been an accident at all but rather the result of Larionov's machinations, and she was trying to find some proof of this in the little time left to her, for the new president was replacing the personnel with his supporters, and her days as secretary were numbered. When she found the proof (all she had to do was stay late, enter her boss's office, and open a drawer, with that ease so typical of the movies), she realized that she could not use it, for the people implicated in the crime included high officials in the government and the armed forces. What's more: she discovered that she herself had been targeted as the next victim. That night, she did not return to her house, which was probably already under surveillance. She had no choice but to flee. Because of her years working at the Foundation, she knew the vast resources this complex and powerful institution had at its disposal, and she decided to use one of them in an act of daring that would be much more cinematic than taking a train: she took a taxi to the Foundation's private aerodrome to board one of the airplanes that flew every night to Moldova loaded with pig-iron. Her personal identification allowed her passage. But once at the airport, the darkness and the rush of some last-minute furtive maneuvers that took her a while to understand created a mix-up between her and someone else, and she ended up boarding a small jet plane that was departing immediately. Just before takeoff, she hid between the last seat and the back wall of the cabin; once it was airborne, she peeked out to get a look at the other passenger: it was the young and beautiful Varia Ostrov, Larionov's lover, who looked almost identical to her (they were both played by the same actress). Varia was also fleeing, but for a different reason: she was carrying valuable documents she had stolen from her lover, which she planned to sell to the Moldovan secret service.

The small fugitive airplane was caught in a storm as it flew over the Coal Mountains, and it crashed into the dark heights. The wind was so furious that the airplane rolled down the rocky mountainside, its wings broken off, until it stopped, caught between a couple of crags. Miraculously, Aria was unhurt. She dragged herself through the twisted tube that the airplane had been reduced to, looked with horror at the dead bodies of Varia and the pilots, and emerged. Once outside, she walked away quickly, fearing an explosion. Because of the ruggedness of the terrain, her hurried escape was treacherous: she tripped, fell, tumbled downhill, the wind swept her off her feet, she sank into the snow, the darkness prevented her from seeing where she was going. It was a second miracle that she didn't die that night; finally, she happened upon a dry refuge of sorts, where she collapsed and lost consciousness.

There she was found, the following morning, by the handsome goatherd, who, like every morning, was on his way with his goats to the healthy watering places near the peaks. He picked her up, carried her to his hut, tended to her cuts and bruises (few), wrapped her in coarse blankets, and when she

woke up, still in shock, he gave her hot soup to drink. Aria recovered with remarkable speed. Therein began one of those
relationships, so typical in the movies, according to my friend
(and I agreed with him), between two different worlds that
are bridged by love. The vast differences between these two
worlds were made even more pronounced by the fact that
they could not communicate through speech. She assumed
that he spoke one of those uncouth dialects that in fact have
nothing in common with Russian. The language barrier was
that much more impenetrable because she, like everyone else,
spoke English, this being a North American production. Even
so, they understood each other. Or, at least, she understood a
few practical details, the main one being that they would be
isolated in the mountains for a predictably long time because
below them the mountain passes were covered in ice and
snow, which made their descent impossible until the spring
melt. There in the highlands, a tectonic combustion of the
coal inside the mountains created an ideal temperate micro-
climate for the wintering of the goats. This explained, by the
way, the goatherd's isolation.

He, in his superstitious ignorance, believed that the beautiful stranger was Señorita Wild Savage, a legendary character from the mountains of Ukraine. This traditional yarn was
not ancient, though it had been around for many years, sixty
or seventy at least; it dated from the beginning of the Bol-
shevik beauty contests, which became a popular craze and

were encouraged by Moscow as a means for channeling national identity and encouraging Communist eugenics. According to the legend, the first of these contests to be held in Ukraine in the 1920s had two finalists—Miss Wild Savage and Miss Civilized—after representatives from the provinces and various ethnic groups in the country had been excluded. In the highly contested final vote, Miss Civilized won, and Miss Wild Savage, driven to despair, fled into the mountains, where she lived from that time on, alone and untamed. (The change from "Miss" to "Señorita" was a result of the movie being dubbed so it could be shown on television in Argentina.) Of course, nobody with a minimum of sophistication gave any credence to this fable, which could be explained as a nationalist metaphor: the eternal confrontation, which took place at the birth of every national entity, between Civilization and Barbarism. The triumph of Civilization was inevitable, even if the people were not at all optimistic; even when optimism was maximized, Barbarism remained latent, whether in a state of fiction or possibility.

Then followed some scenes that portrayed the daily life of these two young people in the mountains, an accidental idyll, a necessary lull in the plot but also an excuse for a photographic display of the magnificent landscape under a variety of lighting conditions. Those vague sequences with aesthetic content, enhanced by the musical score, gave the audience time to reflect (wisely prompted by certain details in the shots) on the great distance the erotic bridge had to span. These two could not possibly have come from more distant worlds—he, from wild nature; she, from the culture of global corporations and high technology. The inversion in reality of these attributes added an extra zing to this contrast, for he was being played by a Hollywood star and she by a novice Ukrainian actress.

Aria was attracted to the goatherd's self-reliance, his simplicity, his primitive vigor, qualities that shined in an even more favorable light when compared to those of the men she had known at work and in her social interactions—egotistical, ambitious, and superficial—not to mention that the goatherd was much better-looking. Deep down, she must have suspected that this nascent love had no future: she could not renounce her career as a secretary in exchange for goats and crags, and he could never adapt to urban life. No matter, she let herself be swept off her feet. Or, feelings were stronger than reason; or, Aria anticipated the sweet sadness of separation, which showed that the frivolity of her past life ran very deep. In the meantime, she learned to milk the goats, was enraptured by the night sky, and discovered the secrets of the mountains.

For his part, he continued to believe that he had found the Señorita Wild Savage of the stories, and he was overjoyed. It was the fulfillment of all his wishes. Though primitive, he was a dreamer and had the soul of a poet. The fugitive of the legend had lived in his fantasies ever since he was a small boy, and this had been the reason he had chosen, when he was an adolescent, the solitary and unrewarding work as a hiemal goatherd, disappointing his father, who hoped he would become a blacksmith like him. There in the mountains he felt closer to his ideal of womanhood, ideal even if he knew deep down that she didn't exist. And now, against all hope, he had found her.

In a precarious high-wire act, the couple was balancing on the fragile spiderweb with which fiction clings to reality. Aria, who was on the side of reality, understood her lover, but did not tell him the truth. She not only knew the legend but it touched her very personally. Her great-grandmother had been the first Miss Ukraine, during the Stalinist era. The documentary details were lost in the successive ideological purges and the fraudulent rewriting of History, which were the trademarks of the Soviet regime. Hence the proliferation of fictional accounts that filled the need for genealogical explanations, which every nation has. And one of the versions of the story claimed that the winner had not, in reality, been Señorita Civilized but rather her rival, for the night before the finale the two had switched identities (they looked very much alike). Whereby the real Señorita Wild Savage had stayed in Kiev representing civilization and modernization and planting within them the seeds of savagery that had prevented Ukraine from joining the chorus of Sustainable Development.

The very hazardous return of this woman's descendent to

the Coal Mountains, Aria thought, smacked of the culmina-
tion of Destiny. She was having a firsthand experience of po-
etic justice, one of the pillars on which sits the art of film. She
felt this justice that much more strongly because she knew that
if it were a movie, she and her great-grandmother would be
played by the same actress (they always do that). But in this
movie, in particular—my friend said, raising his voice in a tri-
umphant finale of "I told you so"—she knew it was a movie!

While I was reconstructing these words, in bed, I realized
that the images had joined hands with the words, as always
happens when films are invoked. But I had to remember, I
reminded myself then, in retrospect, that words, not images,
were what we had; that it was with words that we were going to solve our little puzzle; the images that overwhelmed
me in the mental fog of semi-somnolence could only further
distance me from the solution. I ascertained this at my own
expense when I saw that I had not grasped the meaning of my
friend's last statement. Thinking about it a little, I realized that
I didn't understand it because it could not be understood. It
was obviously absurd, and with it, we were returning to the
point of departure. I knew what reductio ad absurdum was,
but for the moment I still could not grasp that a statement
could be affirmed through the absurd. The only remaining
possibility was that after tracing a large circle, my poor friend
would return to his initial confusion—now from a psychological standpoint—and believe that after all he had convinced

me that the actor was the same as the character. Which meant that he *was* an idiot, and that I would have to relapse into my previous fears and sorrows.

Already, the mere fact that we had continued talking about this subject, after I realized that he did not know the difference between reality and fiction, was an aberration. But he was not to blame: I was, for having realized it. In a normal conversation between people like us, that kind of error or ignorance remains camouflaged in intelligent discourse — unseen, unnoticed, or, one believes, misheard. Once it is noticed, there is no going back.

Moreover, I didn't feel like going back. The images had given me wings, and I preferred to attempt a resolution from a different angle. So I said: "Everything is fiction."

And he, also not one to retreat: "Or: everything is reality. Which is the same thing."

To demonstrate this apparent paradox, he returned to the world of images, though now more cautiously.

The primitive idyll could not last forever, and, as it were, a squadron of mercenaries descended from a helicopter onto the top of one of the mountains and spread out to conduct an urgent and criminal hunt. They were sent by the evil Larionov to recover the documents stolen by his lover, Varia, and of course to kill her if she had not already died in the crash. Was this not the law of the modern story, to resuscitate the dead stretches by opening a door and letting in a man with a gun? From this point on, things picked up speed, with a chase scene that led heroes and villains through cities, rivers, hotels, trains, and skyscrapers, one crucial scene that took place in the Great Synagogue of Odessa, and the dénouement on the Moldovan border ... But prior to all that there was an episode that complicated and transformed all subsequent action, and the previous action as well: at a certain moment—simultaneous with any other moment thanks to the magic of editing—and when nobody was looking, the real Señorita Wild Savage left her impregnable hiding place to search through the wreckage of the airplane. Like a human animal (a beautiful animal: she was played by the same actress as Aria) she poked around, looking, touching ...

But ... just one moment! my friend exclaimed, his face indicating, with a theatrical expression, that he was shocking himself with his own words: How was it possible for a character that didn't exist, or didn't exist outside of popular fantasy, to play a role? Where did that leave us? Was this fiction or reality?

These were rhetorical questions, but only in part. He was addressing them to me, in a very pointed way. For the moment I did not know what to say, so he undertook, with ill-disguised indifference, the task of replying to himself.

It so happens, he said, that between fiction and reality there is an intermediary instance that articulates both: realism. That is where all the tricks of verisimilization, over which

I mockingly assumed expertise, always end up. But he warned me that in this case I should not expect subtle tricks, for this was a Hollywood movie, and not even, any longer, the Hollywood of John Ford or Hitchcock but rather an industry deeply infiltrated by a young audience brought up on comic books and phantasmagorias, an audience with its taste buds savaged by extraterrestrials and superheroes. So, a break from realism was the least one could expect. After all, they had every right to take that break: they were the ones making the movie and they could do whatever they felt like. And, one had to admit that if one was not very demanding, this unexpected introduction of an element of fantasy was worthwhile, if only for the suggestive symmetries it conjured up.

Because in Señorita Wild Savage's search through the airplane's smashed fuselage and the dead bodies, she came across Varia's Louis Vuitton suitcase, which had not been damaged. After several attempts, she managed to unlock it. The contents spoke eloquently of Varia's sophistication and how high a price she had made the villain pay for her sexual favors—Prada and Chanel dresses, Cartier and Boucheron jewelry, lace lingerie, Italian shoes . . . And there I was, taking issue with a Rolex!

In spite of having spent the past century in the brush, she had not lost her instinct for fashion. It should be remembered that her story began at a beauty contest. So she picked out, tried on, and kept the smartest pieces, complementing them

with the appropriate makeup—of which there was an abun-
dance in the suitcase—and ended up looking like a gorgeous
model posing for *Vogue* magazine. When shortly thereafter
she crossed paths with the mountain lovers, a complete inversion had taken place: Aria, the civilized one, the executive
secretary, was dressed in the crude garments of savages, and
Señorita Wild Savage was, strictly speaking, the very epitome
of Civilization. This inversion, and all the misunderstandings
it led to with the gunmen, and what it stirred up in the heart
of the handsome herdsman, was the fuel that carried the plot
to a safe haven, that is, the classic "happy ending."

At this moment in the conversation, and also in the memory
of it that unfurled at night, I realized something: I had taken as
a given that my friend was inventing a plot in order to prove
something; but then I suddenly remembered that I had seen
one of the scenes he was describing on the television screen:
the herdsman and the beautiful Tatar watching emerge from
the early morning mountain fog another young Tatar woman
identical to the one with her arm around her primitive lover—
both hirsute and dressed like cave dwellers—and the other,
the double, decked out as if for a reception at the French Em-
bassy. A somewhat surrealistic image, without extensive explanations, and for this reason apt to remain lodged in one's
memory. This was not the only reason I remembered it clearly;
it was the first scene I saw after returning from the bathroom,
where a command from my bladder had led me. I remembered

it above all for the associations I had made. I thought about how quickly the circumstances changed in these modern action movies, that all you had to do was blink and you were lost.

That visual memory brought others in its wake, all coincident (more or less) with what I had been listening to from the lips of my friend. That said, mnemonic images have the peculiarity of always remaining in a trance of invention, and it becomes difficult to decide which are real and which fictitious. I had been so focused on my friend's words, so deeply engaged in his story, that it could almost be said that I saw figures rather than heard words. Whereby I had no way of knowing if the other images, those that were not anchored to the memory of my sinking into my armchair after my visit to the bathroom, belonged to the movie or had been generated while I was listening to my friend. Most likely, some were superimposed on others, or the generation of visual images had benefited from the unconscious memory of what I had seen on the screen. The only way to make that distinction with precision would have been to reconstruct the plot of the movie, and here we encountered what appeared to be insurmountable difficulties. It was obvious that neither of us had paid enough attention to the movie. Of even graver import: our conversation had not dealt with it as a movie, or a cinematic story, but rather in terms of one isolated element (the Rolex), and by delving into the theory of error, we had taken apart the fabric of the narrative in order to test the certainty of our reasoning.

Here I should add that the mnemonic exercises I carried out in the darkness of my bedroom did not help me sort things out. Remembering, in general, is an opportunity to put the facts in sequence, place the causes before the effects and rationalize a chronology. I was willingly obeying these general laws, even applying them strictly, for this is the way I derived the greatest pleasure from my reconstructions. But what I was reconstructing were the conversations, not the stories these contained. This was understandable, even logical. The two sequences did not necessarily coincide — most of the time they diverged widely — and if my intention was to take on both at the same time, I might very well get myself into a phenomenal mess. If I had to sacrifice one, I would salvage that of the conversation and allow the other to disintegrate into chaos. What did I care about stories! My task had only to do with friendship, the game of responses and understandings, facial expressions and tones of voice — in a word, everything that expressed a thought that was either rival or shared.

In reality, I had never before dealt with the problem of having to choose between them. We never talked about movies or novels or any story that wasn't related to our common cultural interests. This time I was delving into unchartered territory.

When I took the floor, after a brief pause, it was to tell him that even though I appreciated his fine labor of persuasion, I was still far from convinced, not out of obstinacy but because I realized that he had completely misunderstood the movie. Not that I had understood it much better, of that I was fully convinced; for example, I had thought that the two women played by the same actress were one, surely because I had missed the opening scenes and not paid enough attention when they had appeared together in the frame. My friend's full recounting clarified this point, and, for my part, I also admitted that I had been distracted.

But even so, his error was the graver one because it had taken as the main plot of the movie what in reality was a side story, which was stretched out, it seemed, and woven into the main plot all the way through. I had focused on the main one to the extent that a mind trained in Philosophy could (or wished to) focus on an entertaining pastime that only marginally served as evening relaxation. However lightweight, the subject interested me, if only for the skill with which the melodramatic absurdity had been verisimilarized. In its formal aspect, I mean. But this had to in some way coincide with the content, and here would fit the statement, "There are no insignificant subjects." These conspiracies for world domination said a lot about the spirit of the times and, even if they were fundamentally childish, they struck a chord in me.

The romantic storyline, though skillfully inserted, was secondary—and was perhaps insisted upon by the marketing gurus who advised the studio—to the dominant storyline of the "action and adventure thriller." Both shared, however, the theme of the confrontation between civilization and those who are marginalized, or between the present and the past, or, if one wished to put it in more concrete turns, the suicidal cannibalism of power and the idyllic equilibrium of Nature.

With Señorita Wild Savage or without Señorita Wild Savage (because that part was accessorial), the goatherd was the visible and intelligible embodiment of innocent life that was nurtured by life itself and knew nothing of ambition or progress. But there were no more Edens in the world, and the stratagems of greed and domination reached even his remote corner. He was drawn into the conflict, and he rose to the circumstances; his relative advantage was that he was "playing a home game," but the rules of "fair play" remained in effect, as they did in every movie made for a mass audience.

A CIA commando unit climbed the mountain to search for the famous toxic algae, whose importance for maintaining ecological balance and even for saving life on the planet had been shown to be essential. They were a large group, approximately twenty or thirty people, men and women, all carrying highly complex technical equipment. Leading the group was a veteran agent named Bradley. (The actor who played him, I told my friend in a parenthesis because I didn't think he would have noticed, was the director of the movie. He nodded. He knew.) This man—a true gentleman—found the goatherd's help to be highly fortuitous, for the search and communication equipment they brought with them was no match for his experience and knowledge of the mountainous terrain and its most deeply buried secrets. The two men, so different from one another, established a relationship of manly affection and trust that would be put to the test during the adventure.

The CIA had discovered that a group of Ukrainian terrorists were experimenting with the mutant algae for unknown reasons, and they sent their task force to gather research samples and evaluate the potential threat. It was an undercover operation, carried out with maximum secrecy, though it would not have been at all difficult to disguise it as a scientific expedition or even as a trip for adventure travelers. The reason for these precautions would slowly be revealed as the corresponding connections and ramifications came to light.

The goatherd was the first to have any inkling that something strange was going on: one afternoon, when he was gathering his goats to return to his hut, he found that one was missing. He looked for it hurriedly, for night was falling, conveniently slowly at those altitudes, but even so, his time was limited. He finally found it—dead. He was mystified because his animals were the epitome of health. But the plot thickened when he went to pick it up to take it with him, ostensibly to salvage its valuable wool, and maybe, if it hadn't died from a contagious disease, to roast and eat it. He bent over, placed his hands under the dead body, tensed his muscles before lifting, and pulled ... His surprise was made manifest when he stumbled and fell backward. Instead of the hundred-odd pounds he had been expecting to lift, the dead goat weighed five or six, if not less. It seemed to weigh nothing, and when he budged it with so much excess effort, it shot into the air and fell on top of the goatherd, who had landed on his back. As it traced an arc through the air, it rippled in the wind, and suddenly it looked like a goat made out of a piece of fuzzy fabric, then suddenly like a shapeless piece of dough. When it landed (gently, like an autumn leaf) on the goatherd's face and chest, it recovered its goatish shape. What had happened? The first explanation was that it was the hide emptied of contents, but when the goatherd, having recovered from his shock, looked more closely, he saw that this was not the case. It was whole. He folded it and placed it under his arm and carried it to his hut, where that night, by candlelight, he slit it open with a knife and saw that all its organs were in their proper places but the flesh had taken on the consistency of tissue paper.

Bradley took charge. All he needed was one look at those floppy remains to know what was going on. He did not immediately tell the goatherd, who found out by overhearing Bradley's conversation with the group's scientist. The goat had drunk "the dehydrating water," which was the real threat that had propelled the North American spies to act.

They now had to precisely retrace the goat's steps the night before in order to find where it had drunk. The goatherd was the only one who could possibly carry out such an undertaking, and they sent him off to bed right away so he would be well rested and ready to go at dawn. They spent the rest of the night preparing the equipment they would use in their search and to deal with the samples they would take. And something more. Now they had proof that the enemy had managed to synthesize the dehydrating water, and it was urgent that they neutralize this achievement, which would require the use of force.

These nocturnal preparations lasted a while, and one by one the members of the group went to bed to get some sleep. The camp they had set up consisted of several inflatable tents connected by tubular passageways, all lit by a dim, silvery light. An aerial shot made the compound look like a globular excrescence of the mountain under the starry sky.

Finally, Bradley and his scientific consultant, also an older man, remained alone in the command room. Bradley, his face showing obvious signs of exhaustion, took a bottle of whisky out of a trunk, opened it, and poured some into a couple of glasses. In the intimacy thereby created and portrayed, the tone of their conversation became less practical. The alcohol relaxed them; and well it might, for that first whisky was followed by a second, then a third. They discussed the profession they had both chosen and practiced their entire lives, the profession that had brought them to this remote corner of the planet, just as it had brought them to so many others before. But, they wondered, had they chosen it? The scientific consultant said that science had been his true vocation, and that if he had ended up as a spy, it was due to circumstances; among those circumstances he included the budgetary cuts to laboratories and research centers, the vertiginous rise in the salaries at government agencies, the responsibility a citizen felt when faced with threats to the free world, and, in order not to externalize all the causes, a lack of creative talent to pursue his vocation. Bradley agreed: his case offered an almost perfect parallel. His original vocation had been art, and he had also been unable to stick to it with the required heroism. But he consoled himself with the thought that he had not done so badly after all. And, the alcohol having already loosened his tongue, he developed a theory about espionage as an art *and* a science. According to him, it was a qualitative activity. It didn't matter if a lot or a little was achieved, that is, if a lot or a little information was collected—what mattered was its quality; it could be minimal—a word, a letter, a number—but it had to be good. Like expert appraisers, they wandered the globe in search of this precious element, their eyes growing sharper and sharper with the years. They were not searching for a vein of gold, except as a metaphor. The difference was that they were searching for something that resided in a mind, even if it was also recorded on a piece of paper or as an object. And as that mind participated in other minds, and these in still others, the search expanded ...

He could illustrate it with an everyday situation, like choosing a barber. For a man even moderately interested in looking good—in other words, everybody—the choice of someone to cut one's hair was a great minor problem that was generally made haphazardly, and with unsatisfactory results, because of one's ignorance of the mysteries of the guild. A guide for the perplexed might be based on the answer to the following question: Who cut the hair of barbers? Even the most skilled barber might have difficulty cutting his own hair, and though not completely impossible, barbers were sworn enemies of the "do-it-yourself-cut"; and surely they would want to have the best cut possible in order to make a good impression on their own clients. And since barbers knew the rubric, and knew their colleagues, they would choose the best one available in a given city or neighborhood. Not the most expensive or the most famous, as would someone ignorant of the field, but really the best one, even if he worked out of a filthy hovel and created masterpieces on the heads of truck drivers and pensioners. So, all you had to do was find out where any barber whatsoever had his hair cut and that would be the first clue.

Next, Bradley continued, a clue had to be followed; it was not a point of arrival but rather one of departure. Logic dictated that this second barber would have his hair cut by a third, and the third by a fourth, and the chain would keep getting longer because the optimal in human resources was always one step away.

To start this chain one had to begin with any barber, preferably a humble neighborhood barber, not too young (he wouldn't yet know enough) or too old (he would have lost interest in his own hair). One could strike up a relationship with him, become his customer, engage him in conversation, and at an opportune moment ask him, casually, where he went to have his hair cut. It was the only reasonable and viable method, but according to Bradley, we had to reject it out of hand, for many reasons. But if we rejected the only reasonable and viable method, what was left? Vigilance, followup. All we had to do was think about it for a minute to see the insurmountable practical difficulties. Who would spend months working to obtain such a trivial piece of information? We would have to pay a private detective, who would need assistants, perhaps also pay bribes, and, moreover, take certain precautions because a spy might be subject to legal reprisals for violations of privacy. And the result, laborious and expensive, would be merely the first link; it would all have to be started over with a second, then a third, a fourth ...

One had to admit, however, that it was possible. The two of them, with all their experience, and with the experience of having survived, were living proof. That ordinary man who combed through the urban labyrinth to find the Grail of scissors was the image of the destiny they had chosen, or that had chosen them. The fleeting nature of information leaped from head to head, and resignation to imperfection was merely another maneuver in the search for perfection. How ascetic espionage was!

This simile, like any well-wrought allegory, allowed for further expansion. That chain, which would lead through its series of human links to the best of all possible barbers, could be cut (precisely, be cut!) before it had gotten very far if one of the barbers in the chain was bald and had no need for the services of a colleague. Or, by mere accident, for example, if barber number X found a colleague who created true disasters on the heads of his clients, but who could cut his, and only his, hair perfectly because of the particular shape of his head or the nature of his curls. (Though in this case, the chain would not need to be cut, because that defective barber who by accident got it right would also need to find a barber to cut his own hair.) Or, it could be cut if two barbers simply cut each others' hair, whereby the chain would end in a little circle, a "ringlet," to use the terminology of the profession. (The circle could also be large, and by carrying things to their ultimate consequences, could "link up" all the barbers in the world.) They had—Bradley reminded his friend, who nodded with a sad smile—lived through all these possibilities, and those "cuts" had left their marks on them, like scars on their brains.

In spite of my best intentions to move along quickly and sum things up so I could get to my point as soon as possible, I took my time in this detailed account of their conversation, and when I reconstructed ours at night, I went over it again, word by word. It was my favorite moment in the movie, the one that vindicated it, even if the producers had included it merely as filler, or to create a moment of calm to contrast with the vertigo of the action that for them and the mass audience justified the movie. The logic Bradley brandished, though ingenious, was really quite off the wall. But I liked that there had been a conversation, an exercise in intelligence between friends, which was similar to ours. The whisky was a good detail. It placed things in a different dimension, which is where things should be.

Quickly, slowly—what did these words mean in this context? Events happened at the velocity reality dictated they should happen. It was only in the telling that they could be sped up or stopped altogether, and there were probably people who transformed their lives into stories in order to be able to change speeds. But thought moved forward at a static pace, always doubling back upon itself to stop better, or rather to find better reasons to stop. Those of us who had made the voluptuousness of thought the raison d'être of our lives, like my friend and I, watched the velocities from the outside, as a spectacle. That's why we could enjoy, even for a moment, the cheap spectacle of a movie on television. In a certain way one could say that at the peak of prejudice against popular culture, one ceased to have prejudices and no longer cared about anything.

Bradley and his old friend did not enjoy the calm of their conversation for very long. For them, too, the rush of fiction came to interrupt the syllogisms of reality. A noise coming from the nylon tubes warned them that they were being attacked by electric weapons. In fact, the young agents who were sleeping were awoken one after the other with hundred-thousand volt charges in their blood and died with their hair standing on end. The two of them organized an emergency rescue mission, which could not save those who were already dead. They connected a portable converter made of optical fibers, booted up the software, and when they turned on the siren (the maneuver took only a few seconds), all the loose electricity in the atmosphere discharged in the generation of inoffensive images. The tents exploded in a cloud of transparencies, but they managed to escape. They ducked and rolled into the darkness, and when they stood up, they took off running desperately through the mountainous terrain. They were chased by gigantic bearded Cossacks shooting streams of liquid fire at them from their sleds. The scientific consultant, who was panting like an overweight Labrador retriever, took the time to tell his friend that the Cossacks' ammunition was made of exo-phosphorus, the latest hurrah in incendiary fuel, which burned only on the outside, not on the inside, but this made it no less destructive, quite the contrary.

They received unexpected help from the mountain owls, huge phantom-like creatures who, frightened by the noise made by the sled, took off in flight and intercepted the exo-phosphorus. As the fire wasn't interested in their internal organs, they kept flying, though lower down (the flames must have weighed them down). They were so bright that they blinded the Ukrainian ogres, who crashed into trees, giving the fugitives an added advantage.

By pure chance, Bradley came across the entrance to an ancient and abandoned coal mine. They entered its underground galleries without thinking twice. They used a burning owl feather sprayed with exo-phosphorus to light their way, for it gave off an intense white light. Calm was restored; here, they were safe. It was as if they could pick up their conversation where they had left off, now no longer in the inflatable tent surrounded by espionage equipment but rather in the galleries of an underground coal mine filled with feldspar and old lichen. I liked that touch, because it suggested that in reality conversations are never interrupted, they merely change scenarios, and change subjects, and in order to bring about that change the interlocutors have to risk their lives.

They ended up in a huge cavern, the limits of which they could not even see, and they approached a lake of still water. Along the banks, magnetite dust had formed piles of black foam. A regular "glop glop" in the deep underground silence made them peer out along the surface of the water; there they saw floating medallions made of a viscous substance, which seemed to be breathing. Taking every precaution, they picked one up and examined it in the light of the owl feather. This was the toxic algae, which they had been looking for in vain until that moment and by chance had found where least expected. Excited, having totally forgotten the danger they had just confronted, the scientific consultant analyzed the viscous material, mentally reviewed the bibliography, gasped a "No, it can't be!" which refused to cross the bounds of rationality, then resigned himself to a perplexed and awed "But it is!" By revealing their secrets, the toxic algae opened up a path until then concealed from science, which gave access to the best kept secrets of the universe, because in reality they were not algae but rather retro-algae, vegetal mutants with nervous systems, which formed a bridge between life and death. He wondered if he was dreaming.

With a little effort on the part of the viewer, I said, the oneiric atmosphere became palpable. I pointed out to my friend and perfected the argument ever so slightly alone in bed, that when one watches movies in the theater, one's concentration, enhanced by the darkness and the fact itself of going to the theater, takes one into the fiction completely and makes one cease to think of it as fiction. On the contrary, at home, when watching movies on television, one inevitably does not enter it completely. A part of one's consciousness remains outside, contemplating the game of fiction and reality, and here the emergence of a critical sensibility becomes inevitable. It ceases to be a dream one is dreaming alone and becomes the dream that others are dreaming. It is not so much an issue of finding mistakes in the construction or the logic (that would be too easy) but rather the birth of a certain nostalgia, of partially glimpsed worlds, within reach, but still inaccessible ...

What kinds of worlds? my friend wanted to know.

I didn't want to tell him that I was thinking about my nocturnal "revisions," because I kept my little drowsy and solitary theater a secret, and this was not the moment to reveal it (that moment would never come). I squirmed out of it by telling him that I wanted to finish my explanation, and then maybe we could clear things up once and for all and return to a civilized conversation, without retro-algae or exo-phosphorus ...

Or Señorita Wild Savage ...

Ugh! I had forgotten. That, too, and so many other things. So many circles we had to run around in to get to the Rolex!

An entire lifetime, right? my friend said, and when I reached this remark in my memory, and only then, did I remember something else that subtly changed the tone and meaning of our conversation. I just said that I had never told him, nor did I ever plan to, about my habit of recalling at night the conversations we had had in the afternoon. Nor had I told my other friends I met and conversed with, nor anybody else. But I had told each of them, on some occasion brought about by the haphazard nature of conversation, about some of my obsessions or whims or little oddities, because I can say that I am a man without secrets. So, I must have told somebody that ever since I was a little boy, I had dreamed of owning a Rolex. It was completely gratuitous, and I had never taken it seriously, to the point that I had never even considered buying one, or even finding out how much one cost. Moreover, it didn't fit my personality; and that's precisely where the idea must have come from: from that vague longing we all have to be somebody else. What I didn't remember was if I had told this friend in particular. If I had (and in my nocturnal reflection I had no reason to suspect that I had, besides the slight intonation in that "right?" of his), the whole conversation, from the moment I had brought up the movie, began to have a double bottom, and there emerged a new possibility for the interpretation of each remark.

It was a little too obvious for me to start speculating about where this old, never explored fantasy had come from; we all have fantasies, old and new, and that little luxury item was probably, at some moment in my childhood, a good vehicle for my imagination. Whatever the case, I glanced at it quickly and from afar (at the fantasy, at the always deferred work of analyzing myself and trying to understand my life), and with this distraction in addition to the previous reflections, I got behind as far as the movie was concerned. What I mean is: in the real conversation, in the café, I had kept talking about the movie; the entire parenthesis took place in the nocturnal reconstruction. And it really should have been a parenthesis, there was nothing preventing it from being a parenthesis, but, whether because of contamination by movies in general and by particular movies that keep playing while one is distracted and thinking about something else or going to the bathroom, the truth is that it was as if the conversation had continued, and I had been left behind. So, to catch up I had to sum things up and take a leap forward, violating my standard of rigorous step-by-step memory.

The goatherd was unable to fall asleep and went outside. He took a walk under the great Moon of Ukraine, then began to follow a strange stream of water flowing off the rocks. His goats must have also been suffering from insomnia because they had gotten out of their pen and were now floating in the night air, as light as kites, white and phosphorescent. They were easy to make out, and for a moment he tried to follow them as they drifted about, but they dispersed, so he continued to follow the stream of water uphill, which brought him to the separatists' secret laboratory. He managed to infiltrate it, taking advantage of the lapse in vigilance occasioned by the departure of the squadron of Cossacks on motorized sleds. He snuck through the enormous and ultramodern installation dug into the mountainside, where hundreds of technicians worked in overalls or radiation suits with hoods and visors. He overpowered one and put on his suit, which allowed him to reach the command room, where the reactor was controlled; there, he merely pressed a button, any button. Alarms went off, loudspeakers crackled with orders to evacuate, people ran helter-skelter, and he did the same. Since he didn't know where he was going, he went the wrong way and was sucked into a particle accelerator of dehydrating water, which carried him into the unknown depths of the earth, from which he emerged, mounted on an atom of phenomenal size, accompanied by Bradley and the professor and encircled by swirling electrons. The three fell into the hands of the enemy. From the diamond plasma screen, Larionov greeted them ironically and with the classic, "We meet again, gentlemen." In the midst of the general catastrophe,

the security guards led the three prisoners to Larionov's office: dark boiserie, an enormous library with bronze ladders
that ran on tracks, leather armchairs, all in an English Edward-
ian style that was in sharp contrast to the aerodynamic high
technology of the rest of the complex. Hanging on the walls
in the niches of his library: masterpieces. Bradley walked up
to one and contemplated it with a knowing look: "The stolen
Gauguin." They sat down. The host poured out two shots for
the older men, then turned to the young goatherd and said
derisively, "What would you like? A glass of goat milk?" The
visitors' attention, and with it, the camera, was drawn to a
bibelot on a desk. It was the head of a clown, which was constantly making faces. "Do you like my toy?" Larionov asked.
He poked the clown's nose, producing a cascade of comic expressions. He explained that it was made of liquid pig-iron.
It wouldn't be long before the world found out what he was
capable of. But his bravado had no depth of conviction, nor
could it. The laboratory was collapsing around him, the sirens
were blaring, the Cossacks of his personal guard, who were
standing at the door of his office, were exchanging worried
looks. Bradley, who was watching them out of the corner of
his eye while remaining engaged in a natural dialogue with
the villain, took advantage of a blast (the explosion of some
cauldron) to attack them, taking a machine gun from one and
shooting the others; at the same time, the goatherd threw his
glass of goat milk at Larionov, preventing him from pulling his

gun out of his desk drawer. The fight intensified as the walls fell down around them—the thousands of books turning into projectiles—and the roof was violently blown off. Larionov, who had ended up in hand-to-hand combat with the professor, slipped out of his grasp and climbed one of the bronze ladders; above the roof, a helicopter was waiting for him; he climbed into the pilot's seat and started the engine. With a sinister laugh, he began to rise, but the goatherd had run after him and managed to grab onto one of the helicopter's landing skids. The laboratory was sinking inexorably, and on the plateau left behind stood the only survivors, Bradley and the professor, watching anxiously as the helicopter rose with the goatherd dangling from it. But he did not dangle there for long, for by sheer dint of strength, he hoisted himself into the cabin and came to blows with Larionov. The spectacle, visible from the top of the mountain, was quite odd: silhouetted against the black star-studded sky floated a constellation of phosphorescent goats and a parliament of burning owls. One of the owls touched one of the blades of the helicopter and broke it. The helicopter exploded, but not before the goatherd had jumped. His freefall was interrupted by one of the floating goats, which he mounted and rode away on, carried by the wind, toward the horizon, or perhaps to the Moon.

The time lag in my memory persisted, so much so that while I continued to enjoy the somewhat surrealistic spectacle of the starry heavens and the luminous travelers from my bed, my friend was already asking me, in the conversation, what I was trying to prove.

Nothing! was the response I blurted out automatically. At this point, the lag was erased, and again I was in the step-by-step of our conversation and its nocturnal representation, with no images in front of me besides my friend's face and the café in the background. Nothing! I was recounting it to prove to him that it didn't prove anything. It couldn't. What could it possibly prove? The end of the epic in a world that had sold the legacy of the word for the lentil soup of the image? And this was nothing new, everyone knew it, everybody agreed, the two of us included. I had only wanted to remind him, in case he had forgotten.

My friend, with a complacent smile, thanked me for reminding him, because in reality, more than remind him, I had filled him in on a lot of details he hadn't known. I had filled in the panorama, he said in a teasing lilt, because he had to admit that he had paid only partial attention to the movie: he had had to answer two phone calls, one long and one short. Even so, something told him that the story had not really come to an end, that there were still a few loose ends ...

I also had to admit that my viewing had been partial. Not only because of the telephone, which I also had had to answer, but because I had watched all, or almost all, of the part I had just recounted without sound. I had pressed the "mute" button on the remote control because my wife, going in and out of the kitchen, had started talking to me. So, I had had to imagine the "sound," or rather, the dialogues.

It was pretty amazing—about this we were in total agreement—that so much could happen in a two-hour movie. The word that explained it was "condensation," but words also had to be explained. Moreover, in a movement that was inverse to that of condensation, there seemed to be a multitude of events because of the fragmentary nature of one's perception.

My friend, surely taking into consideration what I had just told him about the button that muted the television—suggesting that I was constantly manipulating the remote control—asked me if by fragmentation I was referring to the curse of channel surfing. Without waiting for my answer, which he must have taken for granted, he asked me if I had noticed that the movie was shown on two channels at the same time. Though not precisely at the same time, he corrected himself, but rather, he figured, with more or less a half-hour time lag. He flipped back and forth between them a couple of times, without reaping any benefits other than seeing some scenes twice and entirely missing others.

No, I had not realized that, but now that he mentioned it I was less amazed by the coincidence that with sixty-four channels, we would have both independently tuned into the same one. We could have easily not tuned into the same channel but rather into two different ones, and still seen the same movie. Anyway, I didn't know if this made it more or less of a coincidence.

And, though I didn't say so, this fact explained something else: that both of us could have seen the entire movie in spite of the telephone interruptions. We had referred to these more than once in the course of our conversation, without saying, or perhaps without remembering, that the longest one had, in fact, been a phone call between the two of us, when we called each other to make the date to meet at the café the following afternoon, and we had prolonged it with remarks about our recent readings, as we always did, anticipating the conversation itself and touching on some topics we wanted to discuss. This shared distraction must have also created a shared blank, but the time lag (which, if it really was a half-hour long, coincided with the amount of time we spent on the phone) voided that blank.

But, to return to his previous question, which had been left unanswered: no, when I spoke of fragmentation I was not referring to channel surfing, or not exclusively to it. Experience itself, the experience of reality, already posited a model of fragmentation. Without needing to get philosophical, we could say that this happened in life the same way it happened in the movies. As real humans—imperfect and incomplete because real and human—we were always missing important things, essential links needed to understand the greater general story; afterward, full of doubts and errors, we pieced it together. It was memory that established the continuum; and since memory was also a reality of experience, it was also fragmented.

According to a well-conceived and well-executed constructivism, seeing half a painting should make it possible to know what the other half contained. And reading half a novel or poem, the same thing. Or half a symphony. Or half a movie, right? Though speaking of "halves" could lead one to think of bilateral symmetry, which is not what this was about. It could be any fragment, even a dinosaur's worn-out vertebra.

But, haven't we then fallen into the conventional and the predictable?

Yes, maybe so. But this was about a special kind of predictability, for it obeyed a convention created for that particular work, one that did not serve any other. At the end of the day, art was a convention, and if pushed, everything was a convention. Art was creation, and the first thing it created was its own convention.

My thoughts were fleeting, and I revisited them under less pressure while I was reconstructing this step in the conversation, in my conversations, to be more precise. Didn't I reestablish the continuum of what was naturally fragmentary and interrupted? Because a conversation, no matter how civilized and articulate it may be, is always made up of leaps and digressions, and steps backward, and, "I didn't understand you," and, "I understood you all too well." The memory that organizes and completes them is a chance excrescence, which exists as it did for me: secretly, almost shamefully. Although it probably isn't all chance, judging from the fact that memory is full of conversations.

Could a conversation be completed by deducing the recently born conventions after hearing only half of it? One would have to consider a conversation a work of art, which was not far from what I thought. But which half? Because it could be a temporal half, for example, the first hour, or the second, if it lasted two hours. Or the half that belongs to the responses of only one of the interlocutors. In this case it would be the kind of reconstruction—so common—that one performs when one hears someone talking on the telephone.

My friend responded to all of this with a sleepy expression on his face, his eyes half closed, staring off into space. He must have been carrying out a general review of our digressions, and the conclusion he reached is that we hadn't made any progress. We continued in the same "tic" or the same "toc" of the Rolex.

No, that wasn't quite it. I wanted to retract my former skepticism, because in reality I had proven something, almost without meaning to, or "without meaning to mean to": I had proven, through the positive absurd, that fiction was fiction. To ride on a dehydrated goat through the star-studded sky, wasn't that fiction? Who could ask for anything more? Through simple deduction, the actor who played the goatherd … Wasn't that crystal clear? In a certain way, we had reached the point where words die.

This reference to silence seemed to arouse my friend, exactly as when one has been hearing a constant noise for so long that one ceases to notice it, then when it stops, the contrast becomes deafening. He looked at me as if he didn't recognize me, or on the contrary, as if he suddenly recognized somebody he had thought was a stranger. The expression on his face was so peculiar that when I tried to mentally reproduce it in my memory, I almost failed to find the representational resources to make it credible. What he said when he emerged from his state of perplexity was so amazing (to me) that I became electrified, and I moved into the present. My memory accompanied me into the present, like a written play that is being performed.

But then ... are you talking about the real-real actor?

Who else? And what does that mean? Are you saying there is a double "real" and a single "real"?

Don't start again with your twisted logic. Let's talk about the movie we both saw, please. There was the actor who played the goatherd, and the actor who played the actor who played the goatherd, right?

Just one moment! Now you're the one with the twisted logic. What's with this regressus ad infinitum?

Infinitum my foot! Did you see the movie or didn't you?

Of course I saw it! I saw more of it than you did!

It doesn't seem like it. It seems like you missed the whole part about the actor ... But I know you didn't miss it. You yourself told me about it, about his mansion in Beverly Hills, his dog Bob, the press conference in Paris ...

I was stunned.

But what does that have to do with it?

What do you mean, what does that have to do with it? Did you see it or didn't you see it?

I saw it ... Yes ... Now that you mention it, I remember seeing it, but I don't know what that has to do with the movie. So it wasn't ...?

You thought it was ...?

You thought that I thought ...?

The questions and answers crisscrossed back and forth over the café table at the speed of light, until the questions turned into answers and the answers into questions. In bed, while nervously tossing and turning, I couldn't manage to make them occur in the correct order. The quid of the question was that I thought that they had inserted scenes from one of those documentaries about the making of the movie— what they call "backstage" scenes—that are so common these days when they show a movie. It seems, however, that these were part of the movie itself. I would not have gotten so confused had I paid closer attention, but one does not pay close attention to such entertainment.

Little by little, then all in one fell swoop, with that majestic slowness the instantaneous tends to have, everything became crystal clear. The basic plot of the movie, the one we had both watched, was of the filming of a movie. The CIA wanted to investigate the supposed production of enriched uranium by the Ukrainian separatists and sent their agents to investigate an area under suspicion, but they did so under the guise of shooting an action and adventure thriller, a coproduction, on location. To make themselves credible, they hired a famous actor, obviously imaginary, though played by a real famous actor. And to perfect appearances, they really did make the movie, though they were not very concerned about its quality or verisimilitude, for it was merely an excuse to carry out their espionage; a few scenes from that nonsensical shoot (whose plot involved Señorita Wild Savage and the Goatherd) were mixed in without much explanation, creating a second level for the audience, independent of the first though not completely, because the characters on the "real" level remained in costume and in character just as they did on the "fictional" level. I had not perceived that there were two levels: I had fused them as best I could, adding patches and sewing lateral and transverse seams, any which way. My friend, on the other hand, more attentive than I on the one hand and more distracted on the other, had correctly discriminated between the two levels, but he was mistaken as to the hierarchy between them: he held that the story of Señorita Wild Savage and the Goatherd was "real," and that of the Secret Laboratory was "fictitious." An excusable error, because even after we had cleared this up à deux, we did not manage to decide which of the two levels the dehydrated water belonged to. The most disorienting thing of all was that the entire movie followed the growing awareness of the main actor, an actor they'd hired under false pretenses, telling him he was to play in a real action and adventure movie set in the mountains of Ukraine; little by little, in conjunction with the strange events that took place during the filming, he began to realize that he was involved in espionage and politics, a plot that was not at all fictitious, and he ended up by accepting his role as a real hero.

The only comment I dared make once we'd finished, exhausted from untangling the knots that we ourselves had tied, was that the recourse of a fiction within a fiction should be forbidden. That business of several levels had already been overexploited, and it was beginning to show its true colors as an easy way out, a "whatever." One might even begin to suspect that in our technological state of globalized civilization, there were no more stories, and to make one—or the remnants of one—work, the stories of the stories had to be told.

But had it not always been like that? Wasn't reality, to which all stories aspired, the story of stories?

Feeling discouraged, as if we were infecting each other back and forth and that this was all the result of mental fatigue, I shook my head and said that I refused to follow him along that path of subtleties. I refused to defame reality. I reminded him of my motto, taken from the work of Constancio C. Vigil: "Simplify, my son, simplify." Reality was simple. It did not have levels. That stupid movie might have taken us a bit too far afield, and now it was time for us to return to our point of departure.

To return to our point of departure, in practice, meant to change the subject. And, in fact, we were about to do so when we realized how much time had passed and that it was time to say goodbye. Along with time, our desire to change the subject had also passed. My friend said that on balance he could affirm that he liked the movie. Or, at least—he corrected himself after thinking about it for a moment—after our thorough critique of it, he was now starting to like it.

In the conversation, I partially agreed with him, but at night I had time to do so fully. Above all because there was nothing to agree or disagree about: he hadn't said that the movie was good, but rather that he had liked it; with taste, one can only concur or not. My own taste had not been so complacent, but with the reflections surrounding my mnemonic exercises, it became more flexible. I was experimenting on myself with the benefits of repetition. It is not that I was comparing that ridiculous movie lacking all substance to our conversations, which were pure substance. But the mechanism was similar. Whatever was improvised and stuttered and stammered, sometimes without proper syntax when we got carried away in the excitement of the discussion, I then polished and smoothed out and varnished during my nocturnal repetition. Out of sheer chance, my friend had had a hint of the aesthetic sensations my secret activity afforded me; this placed him and his taste in the perspective of art and thought once again, that is, a transfiguring perspective.

Hence, anticipating my own remembering, I had no problem telling him that I also liked it, or at least that I did not regret having seen it. It was ingenious, and had given rise to a range of musings. Adventure was never completely squandered. Its explosions released fragments that, as opposed to all the other objects in the universe, did not obey the laws of gravity; instead, they were like miniature universes, expanding in the mental vacuum, and definitely enriching time.

My friend pondered the metaphor, but for his part he thought that they did act in accordance with gravity, even metaphorically: because the movie's creators arranged things so that all the episodes led back to a central point, and he found this to be its main value. Not only of this movie in particular, but rather of all the ones he'd ever seen. Not that he saw that many; they were a byproduct of his evening fatigue, his need for relaxation after a day of high-level intellectual effort. Merely entertainment, but one against which those same efforts rebounded, and by so doing, were enriched. And even with the small amount of attention he paid those movies, he could not fail to be amazed at the skill with which they tied up all the loose ends, and the threads of the characters' motives, and made all the divergent subplots coincide. Movies made purely for entertainment were a business; nevertheless, they employed the recourses of serious art, and with the help of some kind of miracle, they turned out well. The most surprising aspect was the enormous number of movies made (that had been made and would continue to be made), and all of them without fail were and would be puzzles. How did they do it?

I was more prepared to explain how Kant had written his three *Critiques* than how an adventure movie was made. Even so, I had one idea. I had read somewhere that there was never only one screenwriter who developed the script for a movie, but rather a group, and a large group at that. This was understandable, due to the huge capital investments involved. The studios could not depend on the inspiration or talent of a single individual, because that would be like betting everything on a single card, and North American businessmen prefer to play it safe. In the first place, of course, because the creativity of a single person necessarily tips things too far toward the personal and the idiosyncratic, necessarily limiting the target audience. But the principle motivation is practical: to tightly pack in the attractions by filling the dead times that inevitably exist in a story told by a single person. Refined after decades of practice, the assembling of those groups of screenwriters follows a well-thought-out division of labor: one specializes in jokes, another in romance, another in science, another in politics; there is an expert in verisimilitude, one in police procedural, one in psychology, and so on. From the artistic point of view, the method has its advantages and its disadvantages. Personal unity of the imagination is lost, and one runs the risk of reducing the flights of fantasy to a normative level of consensus and conformity. A superior, transpersonal unity, however, can be achieved. After all, the solitary mind is also subject to multiplicities that create consensus around unconscious conventions and conformity, and it is very possible that a real multiplicity could liberate energies that would otherwise remain dormant.

We need to be sensitive to these arguments because to a certain extent they could be applied to us. What is attractive about conversations is right there: in the other being truly an *other*, and in his thoughts being unfathomable to his interlocutor. When I go over conversations at night, alone, I turn into the artist or the philosopher who works his material at his will, like the director of a movie who does what he wants to or can do with the script. I, like all of them, have to face the superior unity of collective creation. However, the simile of movies is not quite right because I do not work with cameras and actors and stage sets but rather only with thoughts, and thoughts are made only of words.

Everything is made of words, and the words had done their job. I could even say they had done it well. They had risen in a confusing swarm and spun around in spirals, ever higher, colliding and separating, golden insects, messengers of friendship and knowledge, higher, higher, into that region of the sky where the day turns into night and reality into dreams, regal words on their nuptial flight, always higher, until their marriage is finally consummated at the summit of the world.

FEBRUARY 2, 2006

New Directions Paperbooks — a partial listing

*BILINGUAL EDITION

For a complete listing, request a free catalog from New Directions, 80 8th Avenue, NY NY 10011
or visit us online at **ndbooks.com**